Lee Aucoin, *Creative Director*
Jamey Acosta, *Senior Editor*
Heidi Fiedler, *Editor*
Produced and designed by
Denise Ryan & Associates, Australia
Illustration © Mark Jones
Rachelle Cracchiolo, *Publisher*

Teacher Created Materials
5301 Oceanus Drive
Huntington Beach, CA 92649-1030
http://www.tcmpub.com
Paperback: ISBN: 978-1-4333-5529-5
Library Binding: ISBN: 978-1-4807-1697-1

Escape from Pacaya

Written by Nicolas Brasch
Illustrated by Mark Jones

Someone once asked me, "What's it like to live near a volcano?"

I asked him, "What's it like *not* to live near a volcano? I have always lived here. I don't know any different."

3

Then, I tell him my story. Most of the time, Mount Pacaya is quiet. But sometimes, there are small explosions. Lava and ash may shoot out the top. Then, it is quiet again.

5

That day was different. That day, the volcano was like a fire-breathing dragon. The noise came first. It sounded like thunder was taking over the sky.

7

"The volcano is erupting!" Mamá cried. We saw a huge orange glow as lava and flames shot out of Pacaya. The glow grew brighter and brighter. It filled the sky. Mamá shouted, "Run, Juan, run!"

She grabbed my sister. The three of us ran to the bus station.

We weren't alone at the bus station. Everyone knew what to do when Pacaya erupted. Run! Buses started taking people to towns far away.

"What about Papá?" I cried.

TERMINAL DE BUSES CAMIONES Y PARA LA MUNICIPALIDAD

11

Papá was at work on a farm near the foot of the mountain.

"He'll be fine," Mamá told me. But she looked worried.

I stared out the window of the bus. It looked like a giant orange sheet was being spread over the land. I knew it was really lava, but thinking it was a sheet made me feel better.

15

As the bus traveled away from our town, I saw the lava reach the bottom of the mountain. Then, it reached the houses. Soon, my town was covered in red lava.

The buses took us to a big hall. Kind people gave us food, water, and sleeping bags. Over the next few hours, more and more people arrived. I kept watching the door for Papá.

Night came. Mamá told me to get some sleep. But I kept watching the door.

19

Then, a group of people came in together.
Everyone looked the same. They were
covered in ash.

One of them ran towards us. It must be Papá! He hugged the three of us as hard as he could. We hugged him back—hard!

It was Papá!

23

The volcano took our house. It took our town. But Papá was safe.